Dedicated to Carter, Jaxson, Dain and all my future Băppits ...
Bapo loves you.

And to the child in all of us who still listens for God's voice in the darkness.

—Dwight.

Once upon a time on a very hot day, under the cooling shade, in the hottest part of Africa, there lived a mighty and majestic elephant named Titus. Titus has beautiful tough gray skin. He is one of the kindest elephants you'd ever meet. Titus is known and admired by all his jungle friends for his great, great courage and feats of strength.

Today must be a special day for Titus.
He never bathes in the watering hole
this early in the morning. He usually
waits for the cool of the evening's
breeze. Today he is bathing,
cleaning very well behind his huge
flopping ears, and polishing his
massive white tusks. He rinses
off his body and begins to air dry
himself by flapping his ears
back and forth like a fan.

Titus walks under a huge tree full of leaves,
so he can cool down before getting dressed.

While putting on his tie, he is tapped on the shoulder and surprised by a deep voice.

"May I help you with your tie?"

Titus turns around with a loud trumpeting laugh.
It's Cyrus, the rhino. He is Titus' best friend.
Cyrus is very strong, just like Titus. He has
very big muscles and a powerful white horn.

These two friends do everything together, exploring
the jungle and creating all kinds of adventures.
Cyrus begins helping Titus with his tie asking,
"Why are you getting dressed in a tie today?"

"I am going to go see the doctor today and
I want to look and smell my best."

"Well, you look very nice and you smell like
cactus flowers," says Cyrus.

They burst out in laughter and share a fist pound.
Titus finishes getting dressed when a thought pops
into his head, "Maybe I should ask Cyrus if he would
like to walk with me to visit with my doctor?"

"Cyrus, would you like to tag along
with me to see the doctor?"

"Of course, Titus. That's what best friends do,"
Cyrus replied.

They walk off into the jungle heading to the doctor. Titus begins flapping his mighty ears once again to keep cool from the hot sun. They have a very long trek ahead of them. They walk slowly through the jungle remembering old stories and adventures they once shared, laughing loudly.

Along their trek they are approached and greeted by many of their friends along the way. There is Hugo the Hippo, Jewel the Giraffe, Pounce the Panther, Lupe and Leaps the Lemurs, and Squeeze the friendly Python Snake.

Hugo the Hippo is always in a bad mood, but he instantly bears a smile whenever he sees Titus and Cyrus. He has the same problem every day, it's always too hot and its never enough mud.

Titus reminds Hugo that every day is a blessing and to thank God for all things great and small. Hugo respects Titus and his encouraging words. He agrees with a smile and says, "You're right, Titus. Things could always be worse."

They say their goodbyes while trekking further into the jungle. Titus and Cyrus arrive at an open area with tall trees. They notice Jewel the Giraffe standing alone with a frown on her face.

Jewel is unhappy today, frowning because the
leaves are too high, even for her to reach
with her long beautiful neck.

She tells Titus and Cyrus, "I've stretched as long
as my neck could stretch, even on my tippy-tippy toes.
I've reached and reached as far as I could reach,
but still can't bite that awesome peach."

"How can we help?" asks Titus.

"I'm not sure," Jewel says. "I fed all the lower branches
to the smaller giraffes, now the other branches
are much too high for me, and I am very hungry."

"Say no more," Titus says. At that moment Titus
grabs Jewel's feet with his mighty trunk and
places her gently on top of his head.

"Weeeeeeeee, Titus!" she exclaims in delight as
he lifts her higher. "That tickles my tummy."

Titus moves closer to the tree to help Jewel reach the
fruit and leaves. Jewel begins stuffing her mouth
with all the fruit and leaves her mouth can hold. Cyrus
is below laughing at the sight of Jewel standing
on top of Titus' head as Titus eats the fallen peaches
she drops from the tree. Jewel can't stop thanking
Titus enough, calling him an awesome friend, so
happy that her belly is full of sweet peaches.

Titus and Cyrus continue their trek. Along they go, heading to the opening of the dark part of the jungle. Cyrus can't stop laughing during their stroll. "Ha-Ha-Ha-Ha! Oh, Titus you looked so silly standing there picking up and eating the peaches Jewel dropped while she stood on your head. I wish I had my camera. I never want to forget this day."

"Are you forgetting, Cyrus, I'm an elephant? I'll never forget this day!" Titus joked.

Amusing Cyrus, Titus lets out a trumpeting roar, laughing at himself. Cyrus interrupts the laughter asking Titus why he was visiting the doctor today. "Are you sick?" Cyrus asks.

"No silly I'm not sick. Why, do I look sick?"

"'Well, no you don't appear sick, but we animals usually eat the grass and leaves that God has provided for us first to stay well and if that doesn't work, then we go to the doctor. So, as your best friend, I need to ask." Cyrus says.

Titus stops in his tracks, facing Cyrus. "You are my best friend, Cyrus, and I feel just fine. But the doctor I'm seeing today is not a doctor for sickness."

"Well, what other kind of doctor is there to see?" asks Cyrus.

"Oh gosh, Cyrus. There's all types. There's head doctors, red doctors, even rhinoceros doctors with binoculars."

9

Cyrus interrupts with so much laughter that Titus can't continue finishing his sentence.

"So which doctor are we visiting today, my friend?" Cyrus asks. Titus pauses before answering. "Today, we're going to see a Plastic Surgeon."

"Wait, we're going to see a doctor about plastic?" Cyrus asks.

"Well, not exactly. This kind of doctor is great at fixing things you don't like about yourself."

"Well, that's silly," Cyrus says, "Especially since you like everything about yourself."

"Not exactly, Cyrus. That's why we're visiting today. I don't like everything about myself."

Cyrus stops Titus from walking and looks up at him. "You? Not liking everything about yourself? Are you kidding me? What's not to like? I mean, just look at you. You're big and strong. You're fearless and brave, and everybody looks up to you. Well, except Jewel of course, and that's only because she's a giraffe, and even still, she looks up to you. And do you know why?" Cyrus pauses.

"I'll tell you why. Because you, Sir, are a big deal. How can you not see that? Everyone else sees how special you are. You are sounding very loco, my friend, very loco."

"I know that I'm BIG," Titus says. "And I know I'm the strongest of animals. I like all those things, I just…"

"You just what, Titus?" Cyrus interrupts. "You just what?"

Titus lowers his head, tucks his ears tightly against his shoulders and yells, "I DON'T LIKE MY UGLY FACE, ESPECIALLY THIS BIG STUPID TRUNK AND THESE HUGE TUSKS STICKING OUT OF MY FACE!"

Titus yells so loudly it shakes the ground and the trees. Cyrus can't believe his ears. He always thought Titus was happy and liked everything about his looks. "What can I say?" Cyrus thought to himself. "I really want to be a good friend right now." Cyrus looked up at Titus. "You know God made YOU this way and you are perfect."

Titus lets out a huge loud sigh, "Uuuuuugh! I know, I know. I just want something different."

"So, you want to chop off your trunk?"

Titus says, "Well, the doctors call it Rhinoplasty."

"RHINOPLASTIC? Oh my goodness, it's named after me. Oh, how cruel, and I always wanted to be a good role model."

"Not Rhinoplastic, silly. A nose job is called RHINOPLASTY," Titus says.

"It's still not a good look for my name. Plus, I like your large stately nose right where it is."

Cyrus shakes his head looking to the ground, then quickly perks up with an idea. "Hey, I got it. How about a mask, or some kind of costume to dress you up, whatever you want to be? That'll be fun for us. What do you think?"

"I suppose that might work while we're walking," Titus replies. Cyrus is very excited. He runs off and snatches some leaves and vines to make a mask to cheer up his big best friend. "Okay, I'm ready. Now, what is it that you want to be?"

Titus lets out a deep sigh before speaking. "Promise you won't laugh, Cyrus," Titus says.

Cyrus complies with a huge smile, "I promise."

Titus' ears perk up as he leaps into the air and trumpets loudly. "I want to be a Rhiiiiiiinnnnnnoooooo!"

Cyrus' eyes pops out in surprise.
"Oh gosh, I'm an even worse role model than I thought."
Cyrus pauses looking at the ground once again.
"But of all things, why a rhino?" asks Cyrus.

Still smiling, Titus answers, "Why even ask why? Because rhinos are the coolest, that's why. And so cool looking."

"While I do agree, I am very, very cool."
Cyrus answers with confidence.

Titus interrupts, "See, even you don't have a problem with being a Rhino."

"Well, that's because I'm already a rhino, Titus. I know that I am perfectly made by God, for a perfect purpose. You taught me that, Titus. Remember you read that to me?"

"Of course, I remember. God made me perfect too," says Titus.

"So, why would you want to look like a rhino when you're already a big beautiful elephant?"

"Because that's all I'll ever be. I'll never be adopted by animal lovers as a pet, like monkeys or tigers. Even rhinos are people's pets. Nobody adopts elephants."

"Uhhhh, it's not a good thing to be a pet, Titus. We are meant to roam wild and free."

"I know, but you can look and see lions and tigers in people's homes as pets, *AND THEY ARE DANGEROUS.*"

"And you want to be in somebody's home, Titus?"

Titus drops his ears and lowers his trunk. "Oh, I'm not even sure anymore. I just know that I want to change."

"I think you're perfect just the way you are, Big Guy," says Cyrus.

"Well, I only wish I felt that way," Titus says.

Cyrus has a very sad face because he wants to
help his friend feel good about himself.

Titus sadly starts walking, slowly dragging his trunk between his legs.
He speaks with much sadness in his voice. "Let's go. We still have a
little ways to the opening of the dark part of the jungle," says Titus.

"I'm right behind you, Big Guy."

Once again, they set off to finish their trek through the jungle.
The two best friends walk for a long distance without even
talking to each other. Cyrus would begin to hum a song in
his head but would stop every time Titus would look at him
with those sad eyes. Titus is still dragging his trunk between
his legs. Just ahead of the cliff by the last hill, they can
see the opening to the dark part of the jungle.

With a shaking in his voice Cyrus speaks up,
"Not much further now. We're almost there."

Titus perks up, lifting his trunk and begins winding it
wildly in the air. "Why are you doing that, Titus? Are
you planning to fly the rest of the way?" Cyrus chuckles.

"No silly, I'm just knocking the
dust off of my trunk. Now LETS GO."

"Wow! See, who else in the world could do that but an elephant?"

They trot swiftly ahead, finally approaching the
opening of the dark jungle.

Cyrus pauses, trying to push against Titus to stop him from walking any further. "Wait, let's hold up a minute, Big Guy. Let's take the other way around, it's a much faster way to the city anyway. Don't you think?"

Cyrus is no match for Titus' strength.
Titus moves forward without even trying.

"Uhh, Cyrus?" says Titus.

"Yeah, Big Guy."

"You're doing it again," says Titus.

"Doing what?"

"That nervous thing you do every time we're about to enter the dark opening of the jungle."

Cyrus hugs and buries his head in the hole of a tree, with a quiver in his voice. His voice echoes, "But it's so spooky, Big Guy." Cyrus is shaking with fear. You can hear his knees loudly knocking.

"Okay, slow down, Cyrus. I need you to slowly breathe. Just breathe."

Cyrus whispers, "But what about that mean, scary Pounce? He could be lurking just about anywhere."

"Why are you so afraid of him? He's an animal, just like you."

"He's definitely an animal," Cyrus says, "but he is nothing like me. He's dangerous and I don't have your size and your strength NOT to be afraid of him."

"Cyrus, you know we've already discussed this. It's not my size and my strength that makes me not afraid of Pounce. I'm not fearful of Pounce because I believe that Pounce is no threat to me."

"Are you talking about the 23rd Psalms again, Titus?"

"Of course, I am. I say it every time we enter the dark opening of the jungle or any unfamiliar place. I also know that GOD hasn't given us the spirit of fear, Cyrus, but of confidence."

"But I do fear him, Titus…his pointy teeth, his sharp claws, how he sneaks up on us from behind in the scary jungle."

"Cyrus, Pounce only scares you because he knows you fear him."

"Well, what else can I do, Titus? He scares me," admits Cyrus.

"Trust that God is with you because He told you so. Yea though you walk through the darkest valley, you shall fear NO evil, for God is with you. You have to believe it, Cyrus."

Cyrus begins looking around at the surroundings. He takes in a deep breath, dips his head and drops his eyebrows. He steps forward, with wide shoulders and a brave new look on his face. "Get behind me, Titus," Cyrus says. "I'll lead the way."

Cyrus starts repeating the 23 Psalms.

Titus is amazed that Cyrus knows the 23rd Psalm. "Wow, Cyrus, I didn't know you knew the 23rd Psalm."

"I remembered since the first time you told me, Titus."

"Well, I'm so proud of you for leading us into the jungle, Cyrus."

They walk a good distance into the dark part of the jungle. Suddenly, Pounce leaps from a tree, blocking their path.

"Greetings, my large friends. What brings you this way today?"

"No time for your threats today, Pounce. We have to get to the city," Cyrus responds.

"I only come in friendly peace, Cyrus. Why in such a hurry today?"

"Move aside, Pounce. We're on official business and we can't be late," Cyrus insists.

"Well, well, this is a change," Pounce says to Cyrus. "You are in the front and not hiding behind Titus."

Titus proudly looks down at Cyrus, who is taking charge, not being afraid to speak to Pounce. He only sees Cyrus with this much courage when its eating time. Rhino's really love their grass.

"I can do all things through Christ who strengthens me," Cyrus says.

"Oh, how clever. Is today opposite day?" Pounce says.

Suddenly, without warning, Cyrus strikes Pounce with one swinging blow from his massive horn. Pounce is knocked 30 feet against an old Jackal berry tree.

Cyrus gallops on all fours towards the tree, coming face to face with Pounce. With his hot rhino breath he says, "No, today is not opposite day, but it is your lucky day."

Cyrus is still in Pounce's face, forcing him against the Jackal berry tree. Titus slowly steps in. He wraps his trunk around Pounce to release him from against Cyrus' strong horn. Titus softly speaks, "It's okay. I got it, Big Guy."

Titus lays Pounce onto a branch high in the tree. Cyrus has changed from angry to sad. "I didn't mean to hurt him, Titus. I only wanted him out of our way."

"It's okay, Big Guy. He'll be okay," Titus says.

Cyrus stands up on his hind legs and leans against the tree. He looks sadly up at Pounce who is snoring loudly. "I know you can't hear me, Pounce, but I'm truly sorry that I've hurt you."

Titus extends his trunk to his sad friend. He pulls him gently away from the tree while trying to encourage him.

"No need to be sad, Cyrus. Pounce is a tough cat. He'll bounce right back, you'll see."

They return to their walk through the jungle on the way to the city, this time with Titus in front. Cyrus follows well behind. The two friends walk silently, not talking to each other at all.

Titus makes several attempts of running ahead, making silly faces and singing jolly songs, all to try to cheer up Cyrus. He makes one last try. "This always works," Titus thought to himself. "Cyrus would never resist this."

"Last one to the edge of the jungle is a *stinky binky bloomin' human*."

Titus takes off running full speed, finally looking back only to see that Cyrus is still moving at his slow pace. He'd ran so far ahead of him that he had to go back just to meet him half-way.

While Titus is walking back to meet Cyrus, a loud screech is heard in the far off distance. Before Titus could even react, Cyrus passes him like a speeding train.

"Lets go, Titus. Somebody is yelling for help!"

Titus turns to follow Cyrus. "I'm right behind you, Cyrus. Whoa, wait for me."

The two friends take off. They can hear the voices getting louder as they run. They arrive on the scene to find many of their friends standing around a trap of quicksand. Titus sees that his friend, Willie B. the Wildebeest, is stuck and can't free himself.

Titus moves in closer while Cyrus looks for something to help free their friend.

"Try not to move, Willie B. You'll only sink faster." Cyrus returns to the quicksand. He is breathing heavy and out of breath.

He tells Titus, "Sorry, Titus. I'm just not strong enough to drag a big tree to the sand. The smaller trees are too weak, and all the vines are much too small to help. Maybe you should try."

"There's not enough time to try. Willie B. is sinking too fast!"

Titus moves as close to the sand as he can without sinking. He stretches out his enormous trunk as far as he can to reach Willie B. but he still can't reach his friend. He has to hurry because, even though Willie B. is calm and still, he is still sinking fast. All their friends look on in support, yelling and cheering, hoping that Titus will rescue Willie B. from the trap of sand. Just then, Titus backs up to his best friend. He whispers for only Cyrus to hear.

"This doesn't look good, Cyrus. I just can't seem to stretch that far. I wish Jewel was here, she could really help!"

"Yeah, she could stretch right out there," says Cyrus.

Titus says, "If I could reach just far enough to wrap my trunk around his horn."

"Yeah, then you could tie something around his horn."

"Something like what, Cyrus?" Titus asks.

"Oh, I don't know...something...anything.
Anything that you can tie," says Cyrus.

Titus smiles a huge smile because he's overcome with an
idea, then gives a playful heavy-handed shove to Cyrus.
"Anything like perhaps my tie, maybe? Hmmm?"

Cyrus agrees with an equal smile while their friends look on, confused at their playful laughter.

"Oh yeah, of course. A tie, how perfect. Why didn't I think of that?" Cyrus asks.

"Actually, you did smart buddy!" Titus responds. "Hold on Willie B. I'm coming for you!"

Titus quickly removes his tie and ties a looping knot on one end. It takes a couple of throws to catch it on Willie B.'s tough horn. Titus is excited, calling out to his friend. "Okay, Willie B. Can you tighten the loop around your horn?"

Willie B. is now excited too and begins moving wildly to secure the loop tightly on his horn.

"Gotcha, my friend. Now just relax," Titus says.

Titus tugs against his tie, slowly pulling his friend from the quicksand. His other animal friends are screaming and cheering even louder than before. Cyrus is the loudest friend cheering him on. Titus pulls Willie B. completely free from the quicksand. Willie B. gives Titus a huge hug.

"Thank you for showing up when you did, Titus," Willie says.

"No problem, Willie B. You know we're
always here for our friends."

Cyrus joins them in their huddle. He hugs them so hard he
almost knocks them down. "I'm so glad you're safe, Willie B."

"Thank you, Cyrus. I thought nobody would ever come."

"It was Cyrus' idea to use the tie. That
was a great idea," Titus says.

"I'm going to make sure this never happens again," Titus says.

Titus walks over to a tree and knocks on it. He screams out for everybody to move to a safe place. He places his mighty trunk against the tree. He moves forward against the tree and you can hear the tree breaking by the roots. He pushes with so much force, the tree finally begins to fall.

"TIIIIIMMMMMBBBBBEEEERRRR!" he yells.

The tree falls over the quicksand. All his friends began cheering and screaming once again. Titus knocks down five more trees, as his friends happily watch. Now, the quicksand is totally covered and safe for his friends. Titus walks over to Cyrus and Willie B.

"That should do it, everyone should be safe," says Titus out of breath.

"I can't thank you guys enough. I'm so glad that God sent you my way. You saved me today."

"You're very welcome, Willie B. It's what we all should do for one another," says Cyrus.

Titus stands high up on his hind legs, reaches over and pulls the tie from Willie B's horn. He ties it back around his neck. Cyrus looks up at the sun.

"Judging by the sun, it's almost 1:00, Titus.
We have to get a move on."

"Wow, so late already? We have to get going.
Sorry we have to run so soon, Willie B.
Stay safe, my friend," Titus says.

"Thanks to you we feel a whole lot safer, Titus!"

The two huge best friends take off running while waving goodbye to their friends. They gallop at top speed, trying to beat the sun, because so much time has passed. They still have a little ways to go to reach the city before the sun sets.

While running, Titus notices that Cyrus is in a much happier mood. Helping his friends has made him forget about his fight with Pounce. Titus doesn't want to disturb his happiness with small talk. So, he just keeps on galloping with his best friend to the city. As they run they notice, once again, some friends standing around in a huddle. Titus holds his head forward and tries to keep running, but his heart won't let him run pass friends in need. He finally gives in, slowing down his pace. He grabs Cyrus by his tail, slowing him down.

"Cyrus, we can't just run pass them like this," Titus says.

Cyrus tries running even faster. "Yes, we can. Just look straight ahead and keep running!"

"Cyrus, I'm serious. They really might need us."

Cyrus stops running completely. He looks up at
Titus. "I know, I feel it in my tummy. Let's go
back. Our friends need our help."

Titus laughs at Cyrus as he runs ahead of him.
Titus is still holding Cyrus's tail. Cyrus is running
so hard he's dragging Titus along.

"He must really want to help our friends,"
Titus thinks to himself.

Titus frees Cyrus' tail and joins him in running to help their friends. Titus reaches their friends first. He looks puzzled at what he sees. He places his arm around Zorro his zebra friend.

"What happened to the drinking pond, it's like all gone?" Titus asks.

"A sink hole is what happened. All the water is deep in the hole," Zorro explains.

Cyrus turns to Titus, speaking softly. "There's gotta be something we can do. We can't leave them like this, Big Guy. What's the game plan?"

"You're the smart one, Cyrus. Why are you asking me?"

Cyrus squeezes in on the other side of his friends, looking into the hole.

"Well, not everybody is sad. The hippos and crocs look pretty happy," Titus notices.

"That's because they rule the drinking pond now. Nobody has a chance of getting water or escaping from a sink hole that deep."

"Oh, I don't know about that, Zorro," says Titus. "Ohhhh, Cyrus, good buddy. I need you."

"I smell a plan, Titus. What are you thinking?" Cyrus asks.

"I need you guys to dig 8 small holes around the sink hole."

"Okay, Titus."

Cyrus yells for everyone to start digging 8 holes around the sink hole. The animals separate in groups to get the holes dug for Titus' plan. Titus looks down into the hole. He yells down to the hippos and crocs.

"Hey fellas, you guys have all of the water. How about you let some of these guys come down and have some?"

Titus can hear the laughter coming from the sink hole. Cyrus walks over, dusty from all the dirt.

"Hey, we're all dug out, Big Guy. What's the plan?" Cyrus asks.

"Bonsai!" yells Titus.

He jumps high into the air over top of the water hole. Cyrus looks over the edge to watch Titus' fall. You can hear Titus' huge splash down below, as Cyrus comes rushing back from the edge. Seconds later, huge splashes of water come flying from the sink hole filling all the freshly dug holes by Cyrus and the other animals. Titus' plan really worked.

Cyrus begins cheering. "Titus, Titus, Titus, Titus...!" Everyone joins in cheering Titus' name.

Down below inside the sink hole, the hippos and crocs aren't so happy. "Hey, why did you do that, Titus? What's the big idea?"

"The big idea is, you guys had all of the water. And now everybody has water. It's all worked out," Titus answers.

"Well, you've just helped your friends, but now you're stuck down here with us where your friends can't help you."

"Oh, I'm not so worried. I could easily splash all of the water out of this sinkhole and you guys wouldn't have any water for yourselves," Titus says.

"Okay, okay. You win, Titus. Can you just get out of here and not splash so much water this time?"

Titus yells for Cyrus, who is still at the top cheering Titus' name. Cyrus hears his name and rushes to the edge to check on Titus.

Cyrus looks down on his friend, "Yea though I walk through the valley of the shadow of darkness, I shall fear no evil. Should I come down, Big Guy?"

"No need, good buddy. I think they get the message. I just need your help coming out."

Titus stretches his trunk as far as it could stretch, wrapping it around Cyrus' horn. Cyrus backs up and begins lifting Titus out of the sink hole.

Titus looks back at the hippos and crocs after he reaches the top. "You guys take care. Send for me when you're ready to come out. I'll be glad to help."

They both wave goodbye to Zorro as he guards his family while they drink peacefully from the new dug holes.

"Let's get a move on, Titus. We're almost there," says Cyrus.

They go trotting once again toward the city. They are talking while running. "Today has been pretty adventurous, Titus!"

"It sure has, Cyrus. I'm so glad we were able to help everyone!"

"You're a pretty big deal, Titus."

"I guess I am pretty special, Cyrus. God has given me so many talents and abilities."

Titus begins frowning while slowing down. He reaches out grabbing Cyrus by the tail. They come to a complete stop. Titus sits down on the path and begins talking to Cyrus.

"Cyrus, I don't want to go to the city anymore."

"Why not? What's changing your mind, Big Guy?"

"God is speaking to my heart. He needs me to help my friends. This is why he made me this way. I can't be sad about that. I AM Beautiful."

"Of course, you're beautiful, Big Guy. I've been trying to tell you that all day!"

"Thank you. You're beautiful too, Cyrus." Titus gives his best friend a fist pound. "No offense, but I don't want to look like you anymore, good buddy."

"Why, that's the best thing I've heard all day, Titus. Can we head back home now?"

"Last one home is a *stinky binky bloomin' human,*" Titus says.

"Now, that's the second best thing I've heard all day."

They both slowly walked back towards home
because they're way too tired to run. Titus is whistling
once again because he's so happy. Cyrus whistles
along with Titus in perfect harmony. They walk and walk.
As they look into the sky, they can see the
sun is almost down. Normally these two best friends
are running, but today they take their time and
enjoy talking with each other on this long evening walk.

They agree to take the same path back through the
jungle. It's the path they always take. On their path
they greet and wave to the many friends they missed
on their way to the city. They finally make their
way back to the quicksand hole that they covered.
Willie B. and his family are still in the area along
with so many other friends from the jungle. Willie B.
notices them and walks up to greet them.

"Hey guys, how did you make it back from
the city so fast?" Willie B. asks.

"We had a change of heart," says Cyrus.

"Why? Is there a windstorm coming?" Willie B. asks.

"No, no signs of a windstorm," says Titus.

"Oh no, is a monsoon approaching?"

"No, not a monsoon either," Titus answers.

"Well, what could change your heart more than a monsoon?"

"God can," Titus answers.

"Ah ha. I knew it, that glow gave it away," Willie B. says.

"What glow?" Titus asks.

"That fantastic glow that only God can give," Willie B. says.

"Can't fool you Willie B. You're exactly right," says Titus.

"I trust that you'll follow God all the time," says Willie B.

"We sure will, Willie B."

"Good, so I won't have to come
rescue you guys!" jokes Willie B.

They all laugh and give final goodbyes. Cyrus and
Titus take off on the path toward home. Titus begins
whistling once again. They are just minutes into their
walk when they start to feel the ground vibrating
beneath their feet. They turn to see that it's Willie B.
stampeding at full force. They face him with puzzled
looks on their faces, as he stops just short of
knocking them over. They are curious as to
why he is running behind them so fast.

Cyrus asks, "Why in such a hurry, Willie B.?
Did you forget something?"

"Yes, I forgot to tell you guys something."

"Tell us what, is everything alright?" asks Cyrus.

"Well, I think I should tell you that Pounce came by and he was looking and asking for you, Cyrus."

"Really? Looking for me? Well, what did he say?"

"He says that he owes you big time, whatever that means," Willie B. says.

Cyrus begins to sweat under a very nervous laugh. He balls up his fists and starts throwing punches into the air.

"I'm big, I'm black and I'm easy to find."

Titus and Willie B. begin laughing at Cyrus as he shadow boxes. They find it very funny.

"My goodness, he's so light on his feet," says Willie B.

Titus agrees as he chuckles along with Willie B. Cyrus looks very funny bouncing around and throwing punches as the ground vibrates beneath his heavy feet.

"Let's go, Titus. We need to see what Pounce owes me," Cyrus says.

Titus joins Cyrus in leaving, returning back to their trek home. They say goodbye to Willie B. for the last time, then gallop ahead toward home. Titus picks back up whistling where he left off. Cyrus is running ahead of Titus once again. Titus continues to whistle, trying to play catch up from behind.

They are almost midway through their journey when their path is interrupted by two leaping lemurs. Lupe jumps from the tree, landing straight on Titus' trunk. Titus lifts his trunk, helping Lupe to look into his eyes.

The other lemur is Leaps. Leaps parks his body on top of Cyrus' horn. The lemurs are buddies. They spend all day playing and leaping from tree to tree. When they're not playing, they perch high up in the trees. They know everything that happens on the jungle floor.

"Hello, fellas. Why are you guys coming from the West Side this late?" asks Lupe.

"If I tell you, will you get off my trunk?" asks Titus.

"You know I love you, Big Guy," says Lupe.

"We passed this way earlier today, how did you miss us?" says Titus.

"Well, it's a good thing we caught you guys," says Leaps.

Titus and Cyrus turn their attention to Leaps.
"Really, why?" asks Cyrus.

"Because of Pounce, that's why," says Leaps.

"Pounce? What about Pounce?" says Titus.

"He was here today asking for you, Cyrus," says Lupe.

"Yeah, he says he has something to give to you," says Leaps.

"Well, we'll find out soon enough. We're heading
right his way. Let's go, Titus."

They make their exit, running once again into the jungle, heading for home. Cyrus starts talking while walking, "I really like those guys."

"What guys? You mean the Lemurs?" Titus asks.

"Yeah. I think they're a fun bunch to be around. We should hang out with them sometimes."

"Are you kidding, Cyrus? They'll spend the whole day jumping from my trunk to your horn. Does that sound like fun to you?"

"Actually, yes, it sounds like great fun," Cyrus answers.

"Well, not to me. I'm nobody's walking playground."

"I'm not so sure about that, Big Guy. You'd be a terrific giant swing, or roller coaster or see-saw or a catapult..."

"Okay, okay, Cyrus. I'm nothing but a walking theme park. I get it," Titus interrupts.

"No, but you'd be the best walking theme park there is," Cyrus jokes.

"I guess that wouldn't be so bad," Titus chuckles.

They both laugh very hard as they continue on their trek back home. Along their walk, Titus can see that Cyrus is thinking about Pounce again. He's beginning to do that thing he does every time before entering the dark part of the jungle. He acts more afraid with each and every step.

Titus tries talking to him, but Cyrus only looks up at him without answering. They are approaching the tree where they last saw Pounce, where Titus placed him high on a limb. Cyrus stands up high looking into the tree. He sits back down on all 4 legs and lowers his head. He looks to his bigger friend, looking him in his eyes.

"I've got a confession, Big Guy. I'm afraid to face Pounce."

"Why are you afraid, Cyrus?"

"I don't want to hurt him again. What if I have to, Big Guy?"

"But, what if you don't have to hurt him again, Cyrus? No fear, remember? For God is with you always."

"I know, I know," Cyrus says.

Titus raises one eyebrow, then dips low in charging position. "If you know, then repeat after me, 'I will fear no evil for God is with me'."

"I will fear no evil for God is with me," proclaims Cyrus.

"AGAIN!" demands Titus.

"I will fear no evil for God is with me," yells Cyrus.

"AGAIN!" screams Titus.

"I will fear no evil for God is with me," yells Cyrus.

Instantly, in a flash, Pounce comes roaring loudly from the trees, landing in front of Cyrus. He walks toward Cyrus with giant steps. He backs Cyrus against the same Jackal berry tree he hit earlier today.

"AGAIN!" mimics Pounce. He pauses, waiting for Cyrus to respond. "AGAIN!" Pounce repeats.

Cyrus begins to lower his horn as Pounce's voice becomes louder.

Cyrus pushes himself from the tree, moving Pounce backwards. They go circling head to head while talking. Titus doesn't interfere. Cyrus needs to face Pounce without his help, for God is with him.

"I don't want to have to fight you, Pounce."

"I don't want you to fight me either, Cyrus."

"Then why are you looking for me?" Cyrus asks.

"Because, I owe you something."

"What on earth could you owe me, Pounce?"

Pounce instantly breaks the circling by grabbing Cyrus around his neck hugging him tightly. "Wait, why does it feel like you're not choking me?" says Cyrus.

"It's because I'm not choking you. I'm trying to hug you, fat head," says Pounce.

"Wait, I'm confused. Why are you hugging me?"

"Because you knocked some God sense into me," Pounce says.

"Pounce, I threw you up against a tree."

"Which put me to sleep and made me see."

"Made you see what, Pounce?" Cyrus asks confused.

"Made me see that I was a bully to you and I caused you lots of fear and hurt."

Cyrus has a surprised look on his face. He forms a small smile on his face while talking.

"So, you want to apologize?" Cyrus asks.

"I need to. I'm very sorry, Cyrus. I had no right to ever treat you that way. And for that, I am sorry," Pounce says.

Titus is watching from the corner, he wipes away a falling tear from his cheek with his trunk.

"Wow. I don't know what to say, Pounce," says Cyrus.

"Can you say you forgive me?" Pounce asks.

"I do forgive you, Pounce."

"I asked God to help me not be so mean. I don't like being mean. It's way too tiring," Pounce says.

"I wouldn't know, I've never been mean," Cyrus says with a grin. "I like this new you a lot better."

"You do? So, does this mean we can we be friends?"

Cyrus takes a short minute to think. "Sure, Pounce, I'd like that."

They give each other another hug and finish it off with a fist pound, as they walk shoulder to shoulder toward home. Titus joins them. He reaches out grabbing Cyrus by his tail and lifts Pounce up onto his back so he could walk next to his best friend.

They will be home just before the sun goes down.

"Not so fast, Pounce, just a couple of questions.
Do you know how to tie a tie?" Titus asks.

"Uhhh no, my claws won't let me," says Pounce.

"Well, can you whistle to a melody?" Cyrus asks.

"I can probably growl to a melody," Pounce answers.

"How about Rhinoplasty?" says Titus.
"Do you know what that is?"

"Of course, I do," says Pounce. "Why, you
don't want one of those, do you?"

"HA-HA-HA-HA! Who me? Oh no,
I'd never?" Titus replies.

"HA-HA-HA-HA! Who Titus? Oh no, he'd never?"

They walk until the sun has finally goes
down and there is no more story to tell.

The 23rd Psalm

The Lord is my shepherd
I shall not want
He makes me to lie down in green pastures
He leads me beside the still waters
He restores my soul
He leads me in the paths of righteousness
For His name's sake

Yea though I walk through the valley of the shadow of death
I will fear no evil
For You are with me
Your rod and your staff, they comfort me

You prepare a table before me in the presence of my
enemies
You anoint my head with oil
My cup runs over
Surely goodness and mercy shall follow me
All the days of my life
And I will dwell in the house of the Lord
Forever.

The End

Made in the USA
Middletown, DE
13 September 2020